No Year of the Cat

Retold by Mary Dodson Wade
and Illustrated by Nicole Wong

For Bruce, who finds joy in the faces of his two little girls from China.
Mary

↓

To my little Dragon.
Nicole

Sleeping Bear Press would like to thank Ying Manrique for her
review of the Chinese characters illustrated in this book.

Text Copyright © 2013 Mary Dodson Wade
Illustration Copyright © 2013 Nicole Wong

Sleeping Bear Press
315 E. Eisenhower Parkway, Ste. 200
Ann Arbor, MI 48108
www.sleepingbearpress.com

Printed and bound in the United States.

10 9 8 7 6 5 4 3 2 1

Library of Congress Cataloging-in-Publication Data • Wade, Mary Dodson. • No
year of the cat / retold by Mary Dodson Wade • illustrated by Nicole Wong. • p. cm.
• Summary: Long ago, the emperor of China, seeking a way to help recall the year in
which certain events occur, calls upon the animals to race one another and the first
twelve to finish will have a year named after them. • ISBN 978-1-58536-785-6
(hardback) • [1. Folklore—China.] I. Wong, Nicole (Nicole E.), ill. II. Title. •
PZ8.1.W1153No 2012 • [398.2]—dc23 • 2012007692

I n the misty time of long ago when Cat was friend of Rat, the emperor paced the throne room.
"It is a problem," he said.
"It is a problem," echoed his advisors.

Outside, pear trees gleamed with white blossoms. It was the auspicious time of year, but silence filled the room.

The emperor roused from deep thought and said, "We know the seasons. We see spring blossoms burst on the limbs of the pear tree. We taste yellow fruit ripened in the summer heat. We hear winter sleet pepper bare tree limbs. And yet, we cannot recall the years. We forget in which year the great river devoured our fields. We cannot remember the year that the mountains shook and village houses fell in a heap."

"We cannot remember," repeated his advisors.

The emperor's brows knit together. "How then will people remember the auspicious year the prince was born?"

The advisors bowed toward the throne where the empress held the tiny, precious heir. "It is a problem," they said.

The emperor moved to the porch. The advisors moved in unison.

In the courtyard two swallows swooped in a game of tag. The emperor's face brightened. "I have a thought," he said. "We will have a race!"

"We will have a race," said the advisors.

"Yes," said the emperor. "The first twelve animals to cross the great river will each have a year named for them. With the years so named, we can remember when auspicious events occurred."

"We can remember," said the advisors.

So the plan was set. One advisor went to summon the animals. Another arranged for the start of the race. A third prepared the scroll to record the animals at the finish line.

The animals greeted the news with great enthusiasm. They chattered in small groups beside the river. Friend whispered to friend, exchanging views on how best to cross the rushing water.

Rat, knowing that he was no match for the swirling river, watched gloomily.

Cat, coveting the honor offered by the emperor, sidled close to friend Rat with a scheme. "Ox is slow," she said, "but he is strong. He will get across when others fail. We must get him to carry us both." Rat saw wisdom in Cat's plan.

Cat approached Ox with a smile. "You have such a broad back," she said.

"And you are a good swimmer," added Rat. Ox believed the flattery and gladly offered to carry the two.

On the day of the race, Ox roused his companions before sunup. Cat gave a long stretch and leaped onto Ox's back. Rat caught the tail and scrambled up.

At the advisor's signal, Ox plunged into the strong current. Using his great strength, he avoided rocks pointed out by Cat.

When they reached the middle, Rat saw that other animals were swimming well in smoother water. He feared his chances were slipping away. A wicked thought crossed his mind. "Look!" he shouted to Cat. "There is a great fish!"

As Cat turned to look, Rat gave her a push. Astonished Cat thrashed about in the water.

Rat scurried up to Ox's ear. "Hurry! Hurry!" he urged Ox. Unaware that one of his passengers was gone, Ox sent out great bubbles of air as he pushed harder through the water.

No sooner had Ox stumbled up the bank than Rat scurried away without so much as a "Thank you."

"Congratulations!" said the emperor. "You are the first to arrive. But you are so small. How did you manage to cross the river?"

Rat threw out his chest. "Oh, mighty emperor, I used my brain. I sought the help of my friend, Ox. He is coming now."

Ox lumbered up, still dripping water. "Congratulations!" said the emperor. "You are number two." Ox's poor brain did not register that only one of his companions was there.

Just then Tiger arrived with drooping tail. The emperor expressed surprise. "You are number three," he said. "I expected you to be first."

"I was caught in a terrible swirling place," said Tiger. "Only by the greatest effort did I manage to escape and get across the river."

Rat gave him a haughty look. "That is what happens to those who do not use their brains."

Tiger swiped at Rat, but the emperor raised his hand. "No quarrels today," he said.

Soon Rabbit arrived and was delighted to find that she was number four. "I hopped from stone to stone, then floated on a log the rest of the way," she said.

Next came Dragon. He was in a great humor. "I see four are here ahead of me. I would have been here earlier, but I stopped to blow rain clouds to help the farmers. Then I saw Rabbit in the river and made the wind push her log."

"Not only is your kindness honorable," said the emperor, "but you have earned place number five."

The emperor had hardly finished speaking when Horse clattered up. Just as he started to approach the emperor, however, Snake slithered out of the bushes. Startled, Horse reared back. Snake slid by and received the next number.

Horse appealed to the emperor, "Snake tricked me!"

"Do not worry," said the emperor. "Snake meant you no harm. After all, she cannot walk or fly. She must slide under things."

Horse saw the crowd of animals. "Is there still a place for me?"

The emperor peered at the chart. "The scribe will mark you in seventh place."

1 鼠 RAT 2 牛 OX 3 虎 TIGER 4 兔 RABBIT 5 龙 DRAGON 6 蛇 SNAKE 7 马 HORSE

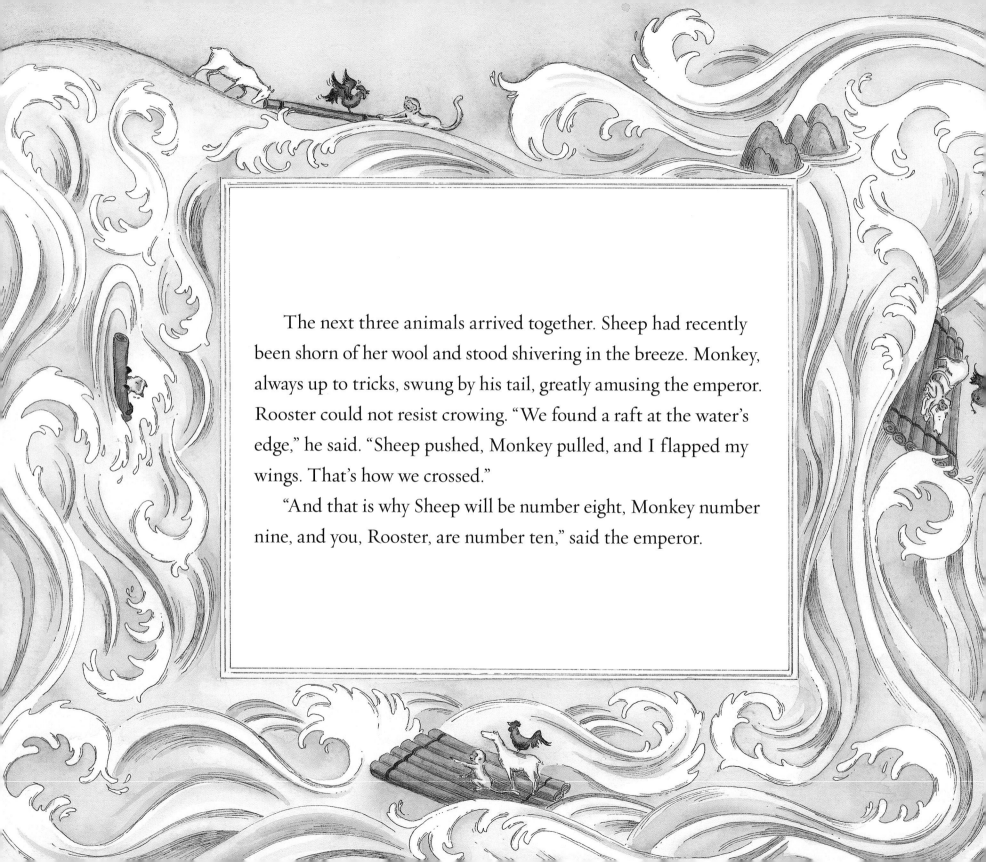

The next three animals arrived together. Sheep had recently been shorn of her wool and stood shivering in the breeze. Monkey, always up to tricks, swung by his tail, greatly amusing the emperor. Rooster could not resist crowing. "We found a raft at the water's edge," he said. "Sheep pushed, Monkey pulled, and I flapped my wings. That's how we crossed."

"And that is why Sheep will be number eight, Monkey number nine, and you, Rooster, are number ten," said the emperor.

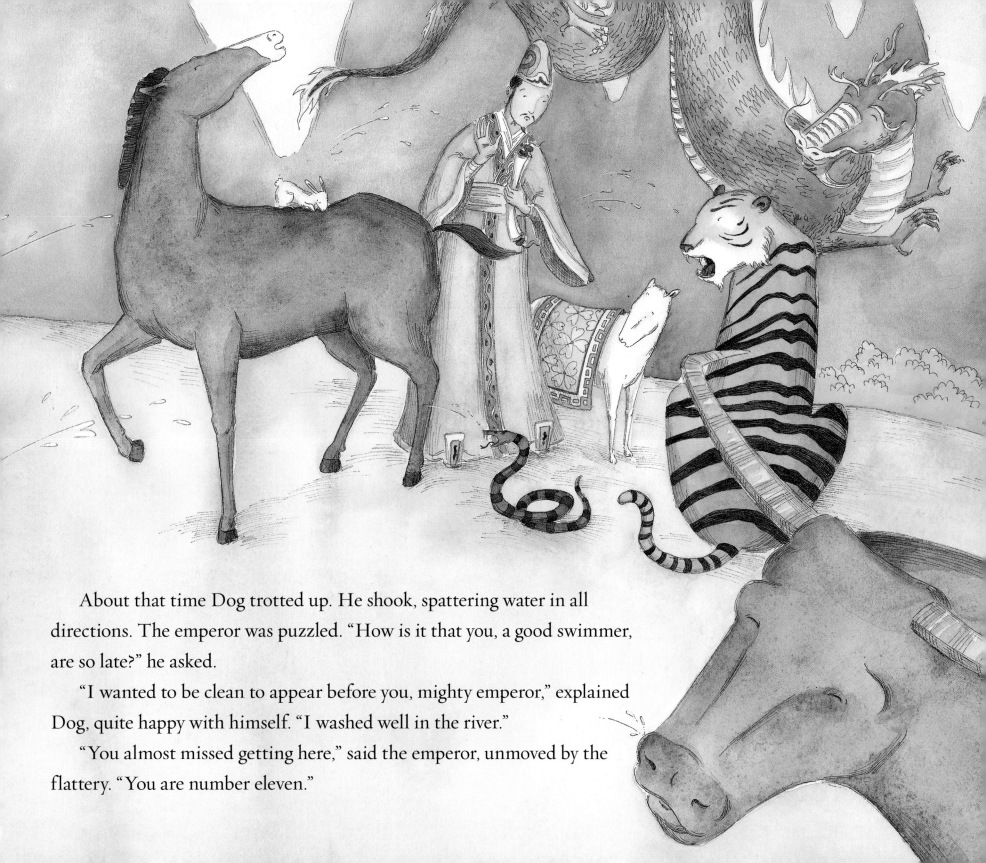

About that time Dog trotted up. He shook, spattering water in all directions. The emperor was puzzled. "How is it that you, a good swimmer, are so late?" he asked.

"I wanted to be clean to appear before you, mighty emperor," explained Dog, quite happy with himself. "I washed well in the river."

"You almost missed getting here," said the emperor, unmoved by the flattery. "You are number eleven."

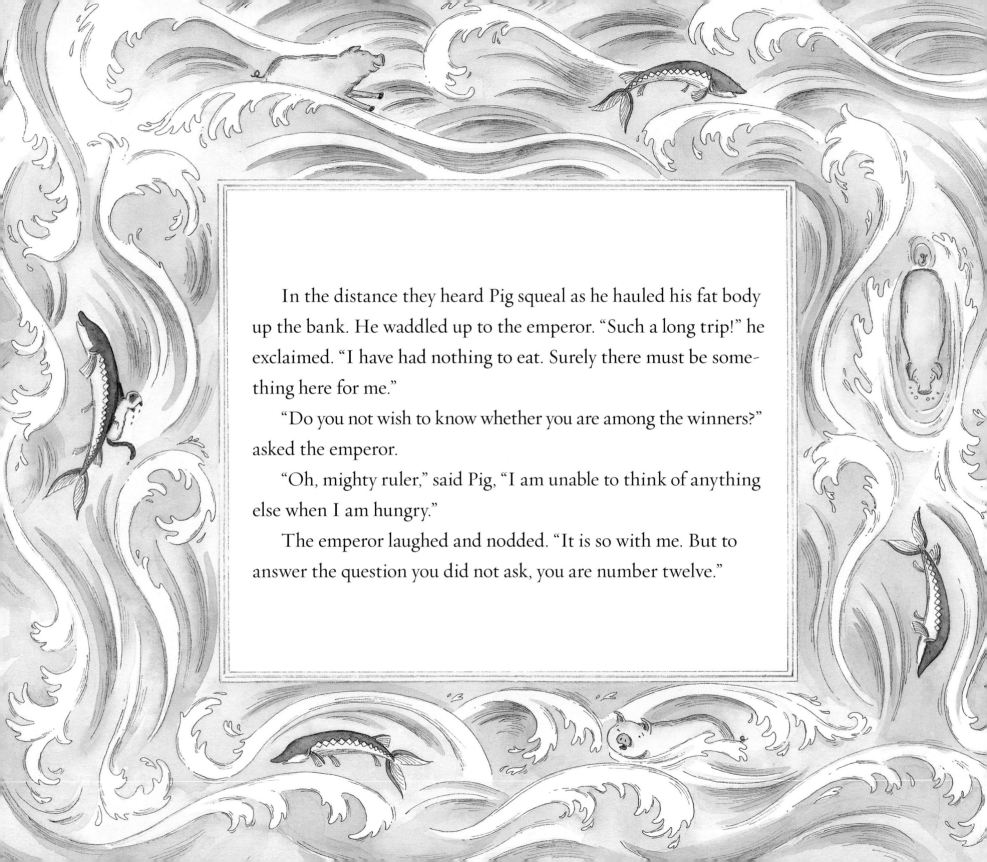

In the distance they heard Pig squeal as he hauled his fat body up the bank. He waddled up to the emperor. "Such a long trip!" he exclaimed. "I have had nothing to eat. Surely there must be something here for me."

"Do you not wish to know whether you are among the winners?" asked the emperor.

"Oh, mighty ruler," said Pig, "I am unable to think of anything else when I am hungry."

The emperor laughed and nodded. "It is so with me. But to answer the question you did not ask, you are number twelve."

The scribe put down his brush. All the names were on the scroll.

The emperor surveyed the animals. "You have done a great service," he said. "We can now recall the year of the great rice harvests. We can mark the year of heavy snow. And, we will remember the auspicious year the prince was born."

"We will remember," said the advisors, bowing in unison.

Amid great snorting, barking, baa-ing, and crowing, the name of each animal was read from the scroll. Just as the noise died down, a wet, scraggly Cat jumped in front of the emperor. "What is my number?" demanded Cat.

"I am sorry, most sorry," said the emperor. "You are too late."

"Too late!" she screamed. She danced in fury. She pled. But it was in vain. Then, turning, she lunged for Rat. Rat fled, barely escaping her sharp claws.

In the years that followed, Cat never forgave. And she never forgot.
And that is why, to this day, she stalks her enemy, determined to repay
Rat's treachery.

And so it is, that among the auspicious years that people recall,
there is no Year of the Cat.

Author's Note

The Chinese calendar is based on a cycle of twelve years. Each year is named for an animal. When the cycle is completed, the names start again in the same order.

The author found this story while on a visit to Taiwan. It was in a book entitled *Traditional Chinese Folktales* by Yin-lien C. Chin, Yetta S. Center, and Mildred Ross, published by M. E. Sharpe (1989). Stories in that book had been translated from the Chinese. Some of them date from the Yuan Dynasty in the thirteenth century.

The basic story explaining why there is no Year of the Cat is a familiar one in the Chinese culture, but the author has added many details in this version.